MW00803748

Snow Magic

By June Eding

Illustrated by Sarah Beise

Grosset & Dunlap ⟲ New York

Text © 2004 by Grosset & Dunlap. Illustrations © 2004 by Sarah Beise. All rights reserved. Published by Grosset & Dunlap, a division of Penguin Young Readers Group, 345 Hudson Street, New York, New York 10014. GROSSET & DUNLAP is a trademark of Penguin Group (USA) Inc. Manufactured in China.

ISBN 0-448-43196-3   10 9 8 7 6 5 4 3 2 1

When snow falls, it seems as if the whole world is new!

What a great snowman. It is almost as big as the kids!

But something is missing.
"Here are branches for arms," says the little girl.
"And buttons for a coat," says the little boy.

You can put a pom-pom sticker on the snowman's hat.
Now the snowman is perfect.

Right before bed, they wave and say good night to their snowman.

Why does he look so lonely?

Soon he has some company. In a little
while, snow begins to fall. And guess what?
Magic is about to happen!

Do you see what is happening?

NOW do you see what is happening?
You can put pom-pom snowflakes on the page.

His three new friends need some eyes and arms.
You can dress them up with pom-pom stickers.

Now they are ready to play!

First stop is the playground.
There are two snowmen on the teeter-totter,
one on the swings, and one flying down the slide!

What luck! Somebody left their sled.
"I'm going first!" says the biggest snowman.
"Look out below!"

"Me next, me next!" cries the littlest snowman.
Another snowman makes snow angels!
He lies on his back and waves his arms back and forth.

The next morning, when the children wake up and go to the window to say hello to their snowman, they can hardly believe their eyes! Now there are FOUR snowmen in the yard! How did THAT happen?

The children rush outside as fast as they can
and start dressing their new snowmen friends.
There *must* be *magic* in the air today!

You can create all kinds of fun things using pom-pom stickers! Just follow the instructions below for some fun projects. Don't forget to cover the space where you are working with old newspapers, and always wear a smock to protect your clothing. Also be sure to ask an adult for permission before you begin and to help you when you're using scissors.

Snowman

What you'll need:

3 paper plates

A bag of cotton balls

Tape or glue

Pom-pom stickers

Scissors

1 piece of orange construction paper

What to do:

1. For the body of the snowman, you will need three paper plates. Take one plate and make a smaller circle. Take another plate and cut an even smaller circle.

2. Tape the three plates together on the edges on the back of the plates. It should look like a snowman.

3. Glue cotton balls all over all three circles—the head, the middle, and the bottom.

4. Now you can decorate your snowman! You can tape or glue pom-pom stickers on the cotton balls for the eyes and buttons. Cut out a small triangle of orange construction paper for the nose. What fun! Your very own snowman that will never melt!

Glitter Snowflakes

What you'll need:

Construction paper in pretty colors

Pom-pom stickers

Scissors

What to do:

1. Fold a piece of paper in half.

2. Cut out half a circle from the paper, with the fold on one side.

3. Once your half circle is cut out, you can cut away small shapes, like triangles, squares, and circles.

4. When you open up the circle, you have a beautiful snowflake! Now you can decorate your snowflake with pom-pom stickers to make it glitter like the snow.

Snow-Covered Pinecones

What you'll need:

Pinecones

Glitter

Pom-pom stickers

Glue

What to do:

Place glue on ends of individual cone "leaves" and sprinkle glitter on, or glue on pom-pom stickers. Now you have a sparkly snow-covered pinecone!